THE MULTIPLE ENTRANCE
Classic Science-Fiction and Mystery Stories
Remixed and Re-Imagined

Gustavo Alberto Garcia Vaca

SAINA —

MULTIPLE REALITIES.

contents

The Second Labyrinth

I first met her in a small library near the Seine. I was looking for the first edition of Boussolle's "Treatise on Human Intuition" published in 17--. Only the first edition has a series of drawings that do not appear in subsequent editions, because, it is said, the drawings and the printing plates were lost. The drawings illustrate the ways in which ideas move through the human mind. I looked through all the shelves of the library but did not find the book. Then I felt a presence, in the next aisle over from where I was standing. I pulled out a book and saw her - her eyes revealed that she was smiling. I greeted her and she replied. Her voice was soft, yet sonorous. She then came over to the aisle I was in, and asked if I had seen Boussolle's "Treatise on Human Intuition" among the books on the shelves. I laughed at this coincidence, telling her I too was looking for the same book and that I had not found it. She asked if I knew about the first edition, with drawings. I said yes, and laughed again at this coincidence. She laughed also. I introduced myself, telling her I was a writer, and that I had recently arrived to Paris to research a novel I was writing. She told me her name - Lia Dupin. I am somewhat reserved usually, but this coincidence inspired me to ask her to join me for a drink at a nearby cafe. She smiled a radiant smile and agreed.

We walked together along the Seine. She told me why she had been looking for that book and how fortunate it was that we were both looking for it: now we could help each other and find it together. Her voice was truly a beautiful instrument to listen to. I told her I had arrived in Paris a week ago from South America, and she immediately said which country and city I was from. Amazed, I asked how she did that. She laughed and said seeing such things was a gift she has had all of her life. She then looked me in the eyes and said she was sorry about my parents. Shocked, I asked how she knew my parents had passed away recently.

"I can see it. In your face and in your walk," she told me. She went on to tell me that her parents had passed away years ago while she was studying at the university, and that she now lived alone on Rue Dessin. We reached the cafe and sat outside, watching the movement of the city. To celebrate the beginning of our quest for the book we were both searching for, we decided to order a bottle of wine. We drank and talked and laughed together, fully enjoying each other's company. Her intelligence was intense, and her humor subtle. I felt myself falling completely in love with her. I sensed that she too felt the attraction. In a quiet moment during our celebration, she looked directly into my eyes and asked if I had a place to stay, and if not, I was welcome to stay in her home in Le Marais. My heart beat fast within my chest: I immediately said yes and thanked her for her offer. She smiled and poured us another glass of wine. I had been staying in a hotel while looking for a small studio to rent. Inside I felt that meeting Lia was my destiny.

I checked out of my hotel room and moved the few things I had to her home. It was a large mansion on a quiet street in Le Marais. Our love grew with each midnight walk through the streets, with each discussion of art and philosophy, with each visit to an art museum or a library.

One Autumn morning as I was researching the effects of light upon human eyes, I noticed a set of newspaper cuttings hidden between two encyclopedia volumes. The newspaper cuttings were bound together: all were articles related to a double murder that had occurred last Spring on the Rue Mordre. The first article stated that two women, Madame Espoir and her daughter Mademoiselle Camille Espoir of the wealthy Espoir family, had been savagely murdered in their home on the Rue Mordre. Madame Espoir was a widow and lived only with her daughter: they lived well from the various investments her husband had made in land and properties. Their bodies had not been found, but blood was smeared across the floors, walls and hallways of their home, leading out into the street where the trail of blood abruptly ended. None of the neighbors saw anyone entering or leaving the Espoir home. It was thought that the bodies of the two women were carried off somewhere by carriage, due to the fact that neighbors heard a carriage's sudden arrival and prompt departure. The exact time this occurred, however, was disputed - some neighbors said they heard the carriage as early as 11 pm, others said it was closer to 2 am.

The second article in the set of newspaper cuttings was concerned with the investigation by the Paris Police, led by Inspector S----. It was stated that the safe inside the Espoir home had been forced open and its contents removed, including the deeds of all of the Espoir properties across the country. Business partners and friends of the Espoir family were questioned: everyone had alibis which were confirmed.

There were various clippings detailing the searches of the Espoir home. An investigation of all of the Espoir family's land and properties across France was conducted. It was found that all of the properties had been sold recently through a third party investment branch of the Bourdon Bank that had received the deeds to the Espoir properties a year before. No definite clues as to the motive for the violent murders had been found.

The last article in the set of newspaper cuttings stated that an anonymous source had helped solve the mystery of the murders. A testing of the blood found at the Espoir home led to the discovery that the blood was not human blood at all - it was the blood of an ape. The Paris Police found that the two women had not in fact been murdered: their murder was some type of cover-up. The investigation of the Espoir properties ended in a small farmhouse near the Mediterranean coast: the two women were found, alive, and living under other names. The Espoir women admitted that they had staged their own murders, in order to begin a new life. They had wanted to completely escape the pressures they felt in their family and social lives. They felt that staging their own murders was the only way they would truly be left alone. Since no one had been murdered, the two women were exonerated: their new names were discreetly kept out of the newspapers.

I thought it was strange that Lia should keep these newspaper cuttings, but I had grown to understand her diverse interests, so I continued with my research and writing. Later that day, Lia noticed that I had found the newspaper cuttings: she told me how she is consulted, infrequently and on an anonymous basis, by the Paris Police to aid in certain crimes of extraordinary nature. She is called upon because of her extensive knowledge of the human mind, and also because Inspector S---- of the Paris Police was a close friend of her late father. She told me of some of the cases she had helped solve. When jewels were stolen from the home of the wealthy and influential Loque family, their entire house staff had been accused and were going to be imprisoned. Lia found that the Loque family wanted to rid themselves of their house staff because some members of the house staff had witnessed the Loque's indiscretions. Afraid of being blackmailed, the Loque family arranged a false jewel robbery with false evidence implicating the house staff. Lia showed the police how the Loque family themselves had buried their own jewels in the gardens of their estate, and that the house staff was innocent. Lia also aided the Paris Police in uncovering a crime ring that had been purchasing buildings throughout the city in order to build a subterranean tunnel system that connected the buildings: the buildings were to be used as contraband distribution points, and the tunnel system would have ensured that their activities were concealed from sight.

I perfectly understood how her intellect and deductive reasoning would aid the police in such matters. As if summoned, there was a knock at the door: it was Inspector S----. They greeted each other warmly and Lia introduced me. He was an older gentleman, genial, yet strong. Lia then looked him in the eyes and said, "You are here about 'The First Labyrinth' painting."

Inspector S---- laughed, "You always know. Yes, Lia. This is quite an embarrassing situation, you understand."

I had read this morning's newspaper article about the theft of 'The First Labyrinth,' a famous painting by French painter Jean Contrer. The painting had been replaced with a blank canvas within the same frame. The newspaper stated that Contrer had finished painting 'The First Labyrinth' in 18--. After completion, he had immediately contacted the Director of the Louvre, who was his friend, and donated the painting to the Louvre collection. Contrer died the following day. In its years at the Louvre, 'The First Labyrinth' had become the favorite painting of many museum visitors: I felt the same way, and would look at the painting each time I visited the Louvre. The newspaper article ended by saying that the Paris Police were following all possible leads in this case.

The Inspector asked Lia how much she knew of the painter Contrer. Lia replied, "I know 'The First Labyrinth' painting is considered a masterpiece of the 'Trans-Mirage' style of painting, a style that Contrer himself created. After his death, I also remember reading about his strange cremation ceremony, where his body and all of his painting materials were burned alongside of him." Lia then turned and asked me, "Can you tell us something more about Contrer?"

"Contrer explained his theories of 'Trans-Mirage' painting in a little-known monograph he published entitled 'Trans-Mirage: Painting Transcendence.' I read the monograph in my country some years ago: it is very interesting and unique in the world of fine arts. In it, Contrer describes how painting in this style allows the painter, and the viewer, to transcend the conditioned concepts of self, time and

space, the mirages we are conditioned to see each moment of each day. By experiencing 'Trans-Mirage' paintings, Contrer wrote, we can enter a liberated vision of the soul as part of the entire universe," I told them.

Lia's eyes brightened, "Contrer's artwork is much more than painting."

Inspector S---- asked, "What would be the motivation, other than financial of course, for the theft of this specific painting?"

Lia looked upward in silence for a moment, then said softly, "What is the meaning of 'The First Labyrinth' painting? What does Contrer's unique view of his art say to people who experience his painting?"

Seeing the direction of her questions, I replied "Many people have enjoyed the painting, perhaps not even knowing of Contrer's monograph and his explanation of the 'Trans-Mirage' style. So perhaps, Contrer's view of his art can be communicated without any knowledge of his style and its meanings."

"And perhaps people could enjoy the painting, even without the painting itself being present," Lia said.

"What are you saying, Lia?" S---- asked.

"What I mean is this - Contrer's philosophy of the 'Trans-Mirage' style is to transcend time and space, to go beyond the physical world. Perhaps someone has decided to take Contrer's philosophy one step further. To liberate 'The First Labyrinth' painting," Lia said. "We must go to the Louvre now."

The three of us entered the police carriage and moved swiftly through the streets. We entered the Louvre in the brightness of the Autumn afternoon. The Louvre was closed due to the theft and the investigation. Inspector S---- spoke with the Director of the Louvre: Lia and I were given permission to enter the gallery where the theft had occurred. Lia walked towards the blank canvas which hung where 'The First Labyrinth' had hung. She stood there silently. Moments passed. I could see that thoughts were racing in Lia's mind. Lia then walked through the gallery, looking across the ceiling and floors, inspecting the windows and doors of the gallery. She asked Inspector S---- if any fingerprint or forced entry had been detected anywhere in the gallery. Inspector S---- stated that the entire gallery had been thoroughly investigated twice, but there were no prints or forced entry markings. He also explained that all Louvre security staff had already been questioned and no clues were found.

"A blank canvas in the same frame....," Lia whispered. Then she fell silent. After a few minutes, she checked her watch and said, "I will need all museum visitor comment cards since the day 'The First Labyrinth' painting was first displayed up until yesterday. I must go to the library now and shall return in one hour to pick up the comment cards. Thank you."

Lia and I left the museum and walked to the large National Art and Science Library near the Tuileries Gardens. "We must find a copy of Contrer's monograph," she told me. We reached the library quickly. I searched for Contrer's 'Trans-Mirage: Painting Transcendence' monograph: the library did have a copy of it, which we checked out and took with us. We returned to the Louvre as the sun was setting.

Inspector S---- met us in the gallery with two boxes of the museum visitor comment cards. "Here are the cards you requested," he said.

"Thank you very much. By tomorrow, I shall have an idea of what has happened to Contrer's painting. Good night," Lia said.

I took the two boxes and the monograph as Inspector S---- called for a police carriage to take us home. Night had fallen when we left the Louvre. We rode in silence. Lia's eyes looked out to the shimmering lights of the city, her hands pressing mine. I could feel the excitement of her pursuit of this mystery. We arrived to the house and Lia asked me to separate the museum visitor comment cards which commented on Contrer's 'The First Labyrinth' painting, while she read Contrer's monograph. After I was done separating and she had read the monograph, Lia quietly said, "Let's continue tomorrow morning."

After a deep sleep, I awoke the next morning to the sound of the front door being slammed shut. I jumped out of bed to see Lia at the front door, shocked, the morning newspaper in her hands. "Read this," she said, handing me the newspaper. There were numerous articles about paintings by Contrer in museum and private collections across the country that had vanished, each replaced by a blank canvas.

"I need to read the cards," she asked me. I quickly handed her the stack of cards which commented on 'The First Labyrinth' painting. Lia read through the cards and asked me, "What did you find in these cards, in people's responses?"

"I found that people's responses were strikingly similar," I replied.

"Yes. And it is not a coincidence." she stated.

Since the day 'The First Labyrinth' painting was on display in the museum, every visitor who commented on it wrote a similar response to the painting: people felt that the painting's coloration seemed to emanate from the canvas. Some people even said that the images in the painting seemed to be released into the air. "What do you see in this?" I asked her.

"There is something we must do first, then I shall tell you what has happened. Let's go back to the museum," Lia said, putting the cards neatly back in the boxes. We reached the Louvre, at the same time Inspector S---- was arriving. We greeted each other and walked directly towards the gallery. I could see that Inspector S---- was as enthusiastic at hearing Lia's thoughts in this case as I was. Upon entering the gallery, Lia pointed to the blank canvas which hung where 'The First Labyrinth' had hung and asked, "Has this been moved?"

"Yes, the day before yesterday, by the curatorial staff," Inspector S---- replied. "I was present when it was moved. It was lowered and inspected. It was found to be a perfectly blank canvas within the same frame that previously held 'The First Labyrinth' painting."

"Was the blank canvas removed from the frame during the inspection?" Lia asked.

Inspector S---- conferred with the Director and the curatorial staff, "No."

"Can you please arrange to bring a large table and two lanterns to the gallery, and then lower the blank canvas from the wall. We must remove the canvas from the frame," Lia said to the Director.

The Director asked Louvre curatorial staff to comply with Lia's requests. Lia asked the staff to place the framed blank canvas on the table and remove the canvas from the frame. As they began removing it, Lia told Inspector S---- and the Director, "In reading through the museum visitors' comments about 'The First Labyrinth,' I saw that visitors' reactions to the painting all expressed a similar feeling of movement, or lifting, of the painted image from the canvas. After I read Contrer's 'Trans-Mirage: Painting Transcendence' monograph I understood that this was his intention."

The curatorial staff finished removing the blank canvas from the frame and placed it on the table. Lia moved the lanterns closer. The top edge of the blank canvas, which had previously been covered by the frame, had a line of writing. The writing was very small and was written in black ink. Lia read the text aloud. "'I wish that every person who experiences my paintings, or what were my paintings, will be liberated from even my own vision of the painting, from the labyrinth of mirages,'" Lia read. "'This way, the paintings will continue in the universe, alive in memories and thoughts.'" The writing was signed 'Contrer.' The Director and curatorial staff confirmed that it was Contrer's writing and signature.

"It seems Contrer had developed a type of paint that would vanish from the surface of the canvas in the span of a few years. This was the reason for his strange cremation, so that no one would know about the vanishing paint he had developed. I believe this was the culmination of his 'Trans-Mirage' style, so that the experience of his paintings would truly transcend the physical world," Lia concluded.

In the days that followed, it was discovered that all of the other Contrer paintings that had vanished across the country had the same line of writing along the top edge of the blank canvas. It was confirmed that all were written by Contrer.

The Beginning and the End

F awoke to a severe itching beneath the surface of his skin. He got up to shower. He turned the faucets: no water came out. He checked the sink faucet: nothing. He went to the kitchen: no water was running there either.

As F was getting dressed, he heard a scraping sound on the other side of his bedroom wall. It sounded like a metal blade scraping the wall over and over. He finished getting dressed and opened his apartment door. The sound was louder in the hallway, that scraping back and forth across the wall: it was coming from Mr. Roeggor's apartment. As F was about to knock on Mr. Roeggor's door, he heard the scraping sound coming from Mrs. Samas apartment as well. He knocked on Mr. Roeggor's door for a full minute, calling out to him. But Mr. Roeggor did not answer. F only heard that same scraping sound. He tried to open the door - it was unlocked.

F entered Mr. Roeggor's apartment. Suddenly, the scraping sound stopped. F walked slowly into Mr. Roeggor's bedroom where he saw the shape of Mr. Roeggor, laying in bed, under the bed covers. It appeared that Mr. Roeggor was convulsing. F knew of Mr. Roeggor's illness but did not know he was prone to such spasms. He approached the bed, calling to Mr. Roeggor. As F reached for the bedcovers to see what was happening to Mr. Roeggor, a large claw-like arm shot out from under the covers. F jumped backward, terrified. The claw started scratching at the wall. F could see this was the cause of the scraping sound. The scratches were deep in the bedroom wall. F reached again and quickly pulled the bedcovers off of Mr. Roeggor. Its many legs scratched wildly at the air. F stood in shock as he stared at what seemed to have been Mr. Roeggor. The creature had many eyes and was looking up at F. It began to make clicking noises. Its thick grey shell looked metallic under the dim sunlight that entered through the window shutters. F could not move or speak. It clicked louder. Slowly, F backed away and shut Mr. Roeggor's apartment door. He stood in the hallway, surrounded by the scraping sound.

The scraping sound that was coming from Mrs. Samas apartment stopped. F walked slowly down the hallway to the fire escape, afraid he would see some other creature in the apartment building. The daylight was falling in shards across the city. He looked out to see countless creatures similar to the one he found in Mr. Roeggor's apartment. The creatures crawled along the streets or

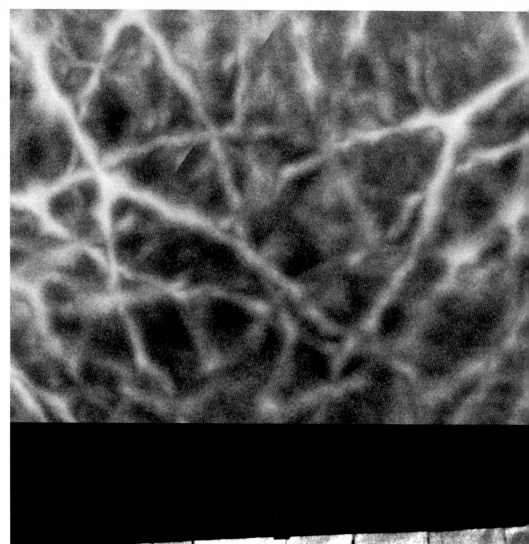

climbed the buildings. F watched as one creature's many legs extended and retracted back into its shell with each movement. Clicking and buzzing sounds filled the street. F looked up: a creature was working its way down the fire escape, its claws nearing where F was standing. F quickly ran down the fire escape, looking up at the creature that was walking slowly down the metal stairs. F reached the street. The clicking was sharp in his ears. He ran.

F imagined what was beneath the stones of the street he was running on: creatures clicking, scraping, awakening. He imagined the miles of subterranean passages beneath the city, all crawling with the creatures. He ran past buildings with shattered windows, doors smashed in blood. He entered the police station. Inside, he found a creature, standing on a desk, scraping at a keyboard. The creature seemed to be stuck in some type of routine, scraping across the keyboards over and over. The creature turned to look at F, stopped, then walked to a back room. F ran outside, down the main boulevards, seeing creatures stepping over the smashed automobiles. F saw a large winged creature attempting to board a trolley car. The large transparent wings on its back restricted its entry through the trolley doors. The creature finally stopped its attempts: the trolley doors closed. The empty trolley began moving down the boulevard. The creature's wings began to flap, the buzzing sound causing F to cringe in pain. F watched as the creature flew above him, directionless. It then appeared to notice something and flew down a side street.

F ran past rows of bent metal and broken glass. Scraps of ripped clothing and paper fluttered in the wind. He ran into smashed store fronts: everything had been destroyed, ripped apart. He heard a multitude of chattering sounds nearby. He reached the city center. The chattering sounds were all coming from the central square. He remembered that the market was held there midweek. F stepped across small pools of mashed fruits, vegetables and blood as he approached the square. The chattering sounds grew louder until he reached the square. The smells made F feel ill. Hundreds of creatures were swarming in the square: fighting and killing each other to eat the scraps of fruits and vegetables scattered across the square. Creatures were eating or defending their food. Some creatures were climbing away with small morsels in their claws. Some creatures were dying, wheezing sounds emanating from inside their shells.

Night fell across the city. The lights were on in the government building where F worked. He ran in. Every room was in disarray. The building appeared to be empty of the creatures. F thought of trying to reach someone, to tell of what was happening. He tried all modes of communication - everything was static. F walked to his desk and sat, taking out a sheet of paper. He began to write. He wrote for hours. When he stopped to read what he had written, he saw only unintelligible marks on the paper. He felt a sharp itching on his face. He scratched at it as he tried to understand what he had written on the paper. The itching grew more intense as he scratched and scraped at his face. Slices of his skin started to fall onto the desk. The office lights were reflected in his thick grey shell.

Sahrazad

Each night, the boy would run excitedly to the central hall of the city. He had finished all of his school work and completed the cleaning chores his mother had assigned him that day, so she would allow him to walk (although he would always run) alone to the central hall. He was thankful to have such an understanding mother and would always tell her the stories he had heard that day as soon as he returned home. She would listen as she worked, drawing new designs for a gown or sewing intricate patterns of beads onto a dress.

Each night the boy would approach the central hall doors with a deep reverence. This was the place where dreams and visions were brought forth. He would look into the designs of the doors, his eyes following the lines carved in wood. He would enter the central hall courtyard and sit by the entrance doors, inhaling the sweet fragrance of the jasmine flowers that extended along the walls of the courtyard.

He would watch the stars move across in the sky. Soon, others would enter and they would all joyfully greet each other and eagerly discuss the previous night's stories and anticipate the next stories.

As the moon would become visible in the courtyard, Sahrazad the storyteller, would arrive.

The oil lamps that hung in the courtyard would give off a dim, blue light.

Sahrazad would begin to sway in the soft light, her voice floating in the night air.

She would tell stories of magical beings and distant islands, of kings and princesses. Of labyrinths and oceans. Of animals who wanted to be more than what they were. Stories of beggars who were actually kings in hiding, of forests where birds speak in human voices. Of cities built for spirits to inhabit. Of towers where the mysteries of the past are stored.

The boy would close his eyes and visualize the worlds she told of. He would open his eyes and see her hands moving across the night sky as she spoke, her gestures forming paintings in the air.

One night, after Sahrazad had told that night's tales and everyone was laughing and smiling as they exited the courtyard, Sahrazad approached the boy and gave him a book. He thanked her happily and accepted the gift, looking through its many pages. But there was nothing written on any page of the book. He asked her why the book was blank. She smiled and told him the book is for him to fill with everything he can imagine, because the book is as infinite as our minds.

The Spreading Virus

The sun had set in a haze above the city. The cold winter night was casting a dense fog over the network of streets and roadways of the city. Horse-drawn cabs appeared suddenly through the haze. Soft voices fluttered in and out of the thick greyness. The fog wrapped itself tighter around the streets. I had an uneasy feeling within me. Maybe it was a premonition. Maybe it was the effect this city was having on my mind.

I was thankful to finally reach Baker Street. I entered Holmes' room and found him sitting in silence, overlooking the movement of people outside of his window. He watched as they moved towards their destinations, meetings or appointments. He usually enjoyed deducing people's destinations from their walk, or what they were carrying, or the expressions on their faces. That day, however, was different: he seemed saddened as his eyes followed the couple smiling arm in arm, or the gentleman walking purposefully down the street, or the young woman in a new dress.

"What is wrong, Holmes?" I asked quietly.

"Wrong? What is wrong.... What is wrong.... or right? Watson, I have dedicated my life to delineating between wrong and right, between a just life and a criminal life. Tonight, I'm afraid, that delineation, that line I have endeavored to mark, will be severed," he stated, looking up at me with a growing darkness in his eyes.

"What do you mean? How?" I queried, sitting across from him. I had never seen my friend in this state.

"When someone gets an illness, a fever, let's say, it would not be considered that person's fault that he or she fell ill. That person is not to blame for the sickness that befell him or her."

"Of course not. We have no choice whether or not we get ill. We have little control over the viruses that surround us."

"Exactly. Exactly. And subsequently, if we think of a thought, an evil thought, as a virus, as moving and spreading in the same ways as a virus, then that thought can spread as infectiously as the worst plague humanity has ever encountered."

"Holmes, I truly do not understand what has you in this state. What has occurred to have you thinking of such things?"

"Don't you see, Watson? A mere thought can be just as serious as the most vile plague. And who is to blame...?" Holmes said, his voice becoming nearly a whisper. I did not respond. I sat quietly, trying to ascertain why my friend would be in such a state. He had solved all of his recent cases successfully. I could see that he had not fallen ill and that he was not in any danger that I knew of. My thoughts turned to how little I actually knew of Holmes' past when he suddenly cried out, "There is a growing plague in this city! A plague that must be eradicated so that it never returns!"

He saw my look of astonishment and continued, calmer, "Watson, you must understand. As a doctor, and my colleague, you must appreciate the fact that we have traversed some of the depths that humans are capable of descending. Now I see why. Now I see that the criminal motivations that are encircling this city, and soon the world, are all born from one thought, one virus. At first, as you recall, I believed it all to be the work of Professor Moriarty and his intricate system of criminals and duplicitous politicians and corrupt police officers. But after his demise, and our work to destroy his network, the evil still lingers. This plague, this evil, is worse than a thousand Moriartys! And tonight, in approximately one minute, we shall meet the one who is responsible for this spreading plague."

I gasped and reached for my pistol.

"You do well to arm yourself. I too am prepared. But there is something else you must understand. Eradicating him is only the beginning."

The knock at the door startled me. With pistol in hand, I answered the door. A tall stranger was standing alone in the dark doorway. His tall frame was outlined by the grey fog behind him. He put his hands in the air, saying, "Good evening. I trust you received my telegram confirming our meeting."

I ensured he was not armed and allowed him to enter. Holmes stood up quickly, looking him over as he entered. He was an older gentleman, dressed in the finest clothes: all of the materials were imported and perfectly tailored to his height. His facial features were distinct, but are now difficult to recall.

"Yes. I appreciate your prompt arrival," Holmes said.

"I must say that your request to meet was quite a surprise. I had no idea I was so transparent. I did not realize that I could be found so quickly. But then, your reputation as a detective is known throughout the world."

"And your reputation is just as vast, although no one knows you by name."

"Yes, I mean to ask you: how did you discover my name?" the stranger asked, sitting down.

I stood there, uncertain of what to do. Holmes saw my uneasiness and motioned for me to sit.

"Your name, although I know it is not your true name, took days of decoding. Knowing your involvement in printing industries and information networks, I used literary characters, and inversions of names found in daily newspapers, and ancient city names. Once I decoded your present name, I began decoding where I might find you. And knowing your tastes, I knew that you would be wintering among the mountains of the Continent. Narrowing the possibilities of which town you were in was a simple matter of finding the resort towns where your types play," Holmes stated.

"My types? That's interesting," the stranger smiled.

"When I say your types, I am referring merely to the fact that the only type of person to be found where I found you, is the type of person who winters in mountain lodges and summers in distant islands - all while crushing the lives of others to live such a life," Holmes replied coolly. "I have called you to this meeting so that you know - I now see that every time there is an unsolved murder or a missing person or the beginnings of a war, you are involved. I have grown to understand that your influence is as wide as the planet itself. I now see that all of these crimes serve to spread your virus, your...plague."

"I see that I have not erred in coming here. This is quite entertaining," the stranger laughed, throwing himself through the window. I rushed to the window.

Holmes shouted, "Shoot, Watson!" I aimed and fired but the night fog was too thick: I heard the bullets hit the wall of the corner building. The stranger ran down the street, his laughter echoing in the night air.

We grabbed our lanterns and ran after him. Our lanterns gave off diffused light, which helped us very little. Street lamps burned weakly in the fog. Holmes relied on his sharp sense of hearing, which guided us through the sequence of streets and alleys as the stranger's laughter lingered in the night air. We caught sight of his tall shape, running toward the bridge that towers over the river. There were too many pedestrians to take a clear shot at him.

"Don't worry, Watson. You'll get your chance," Holmes told me. We reached the bridge, the lights of its towers barely visible in the fog. We heard his footsteps running to the center of the bridge. Holmes stopped and listened. Hearing only the stranger's breath on the bridge, he pulled out his silver throwing knife and released it into the fog at the center of the bridge. We heard only the scraping of the knife on the stone of the bridge, and the stranger's laughter.

"Fire now, Watson!" Holmes shouted. I shot twice and heard both shots hit only stone. Surprised, we ran towards the center of the bridge and found him standing, unhurt.

"You are both truly excellent marksmen, but you are still only men. Men of limited influence," the stranger smiled.

Holmes looked at him in the eyes, "In your eyes it may be limited, because we do not speak to the greed or frailty of humanity as you do."

"And that is precisely your problem. You view criminal thought as evil, and you call it a virus - but viruses have no morality. Every person alive, all those you classify as either good or evil, is subject to the same viruses, the same illnesses, that move across the earth. Your doctor friend can attest to that. As you have correctly deduced, the virus is spreading. Read the newspapers, or any novel. Go see a play, or listen to a concert. It is there, between the words. The virus that you speak of is there: it has been there since the beginning, and it will continue to be there, long after our meeting on this bridge, on this night, at this time. What you fail to comprehend is that the cause of the virus is within."

Holmes looked at him with deep rage, saying, "It is fitting, then, that we should end this meeting on a bridge which connects what was once divided."

Holmes swiftly removed another silver throwing knife from its strap and threw it directly towards the stranger's forehead. Just then a gust of wind blew, covering all three of us in a thick fog. Again, the only sound we heard was the scraping of knife metal on the stone of the bridge. I rushed to where the stranger had been standing: he was not there. The stranger had disappeared in the fog. I looked all across the bridge and found no one.

Holmes has never told me the name, or identity, of the stranger.

The Eclipse Within

The sky over the small town was reflected in the waters of the river. Fall was approaching.

The people of the town gathered outside the town hall as they did every Friday evening. They talked and laughed and gossiped, children ran through the crowd, playing and chasing each other.

Suddenly someone gasped - the mayor, who was walking slowly in his usual meditative way, had something strange over his face.

Everyone turned to look at the mayor. Tied around his forehead, and hanging down over his entire face, the mayor had on a black veil. It was made of crape, entirely concealing his features, down to his mouth and chin.

The mayor was not an eccentric man by any means. He was a well-respected person in town as a citizen, and as their representative and leader. This made his strange new appearance such a shock to the people in the town.

He walked onward, at a slow and quiet pace, nodding to the town council members who stood on the town hall steps. The council members were so shocked they could barely respond to his greeting.

Everyone whispered and looked at each other, confused at the mayor's appearance. A woman commented on how strange that a black veil, common on a woman's face, became such a frightening thing on the mayor's face.

The crowd entered the town hall with a muffled commotion and speculation at the mayor's look.

The mayor appeared not to notice the confusion of the people. He walked through the town hall almost without sound, ascended the stairs, and stood at the podium overlooking the crowd and the council members as they all sat.

He did not take off his black veil. He addressed the town, as he always did on Friday evenings, discussing the events of the week and plans of the future for their small but growing town.

He then began to speak in a tone the townspeople had not heard before. A sharp clarity was in his voice. He spoke with an urgency of action. He did not speak loudly, but his voice seemed to echo through the hall, out into the town roads and across the hills.

He spoke of how all people of the town, and all the people around the world, must look past their inner prejudices. He spoke of how all people must work together to create a place where all people could be happy. He spoke of building a world where there is hope.

The black veil, hanging down from his forehead to his mouth, moved as he spoke, but was never lifted from his face. Each member of the crowd - an innocent girl, a reformed criminal, a divorced

mother, an elderly man - felt as if the mayor had discovered something hidden deep inside of them and that he was speaking directly to their very souls. There was nothing accusatory in what the mayor said, and yet, with every word, the townspeople quaked.

Then he addressed the very thing that was on all of the townspeople's minds: he spoke of how one day all people must remove their own black veils. He stated that if the black veil is a sign of fear, then one day a black veil will not be necessary because there will be no fear. If the black veil is a sign of sorrow, then one day it will not be necessary because there will be no sorrow. If the black veil is a sign of mourning, then one day it will not be necessary because there will be no mourning. He stated that it is possible to build a world where truth and honesty can be seen on every person's face.

He calmly thanked the town for their attention, as he always did, and moved to leave the town hall by the side door. Before exiting, he looked back at the townspeople, all of whom had their eyes fixed on him. A sad smile flickered from beneath the black veil, glimmering as he disappeared in the night.

After his town hall address, the townspeople rushed out of the town hall. Some gathered together, whispering. Some went home, walking meditatively. Some talked loudly, and spoke against politics and politicians.

The following day, the whole town talked of little else than the mayor's black veil. That, and the mysterious words of the mayor's speech, were the topics for discussion between acquaintances meeting in the street, and women gossiping at their open windows, and children talking on their way to school.

That day, many curious people came calling to the mayor's office: all were greeted only by a sheet of paper hanging on the office door. On the paper, in the mayor's own writing, was the text of the speech that he had given the night before. The mayor was never seen again.

The mayor was always remembered by the townspeople as a kind and caring person, but the strange words he spoke on the day he wore the black veil continued to resonate in the minds of the townspeople.

It was rumored that the mayor moved to a distant town and that he never said a word for the rest of his life.

It was said that nothing, not even the wind, moved aside the black veil from his face until he passed quietly, alone, into the next world.

The Illuminated Bridge

The person who built the bridge has been forgotten.

The bridge crosses the wide, quiet river, connecting the small town to the hills on the eastern edge of the town.

It has been said that the original plans for the bridge were kept in a small temple in the hills: the temple was destroyed by a fire many years ago.

In the past, townspeople would frequently cross the bridge, entering the forest in the hills to cut trees or to hunt.

Recently, a young woman was seen crossing the bridge after midnight. She was carrying a lantern and walking slowly by herself. The night was foggy, so the few people who saw her say they only saw the outline of her shape in the dim light of her lantern. Then they heard a scream and saw the lantern light go out.

After that night, anyone trying to cross the bridge to reach the forest is strongly repelled by an unknown force. The force has been described as a young woman's hands pushing upon one's chest.

And each night, sometime after midnight, the center of the bridge is illuminated. The light lasts for a few minutes, or sometimes for an hour, then is extinguished.

The townspeople's fear has caused them to stop using the bridge. In the day, a strange light can be seen in the forest beyond the bridge.

Once, a group of men of the town decided to battle the force that they believed was on the bridge, or in the trees beyond the bridge.

They stood together on the town side of the bridge, their weapons in their hands, waiting.

After midnight, they saw the shape of a young woman walking towards the center of the bridge, carrying a lantern. She was in a flowing white dress. They could not see her clearly through the mists of the river.

In the light of her lantern, they watched as she approached the center of the bridge. Her long black hair covered her face.

Then they saw the forms of many figures walking from the hills, through the trees and onto the bridge.

The men cautiously walked onto the bridge, towards the center, where the young woman stood, unmoving. Suddenly, she stretched her lantern over the bridge illuminating the water below.

The men, afraid and unable to move further, watched as the figures moved toward the light at the center of the bridge: the young men saw that all of the figures were faceless.

One by one, the faceless figures dissipated in the thin rays of the lantern, falling in wisps of light onto the surface of the quiet river.

The young woman turned towards the men and screamed, her lantern going out.

Since then, no one else in the town has tried to cross the bridge. The townspeople have found other sources of food and wood.

The bridge still stands, unused by the townspeople.

It is said that the bridge continues to be illuminated each night after midnight. Some say they can hear a young woman's scream across the river.

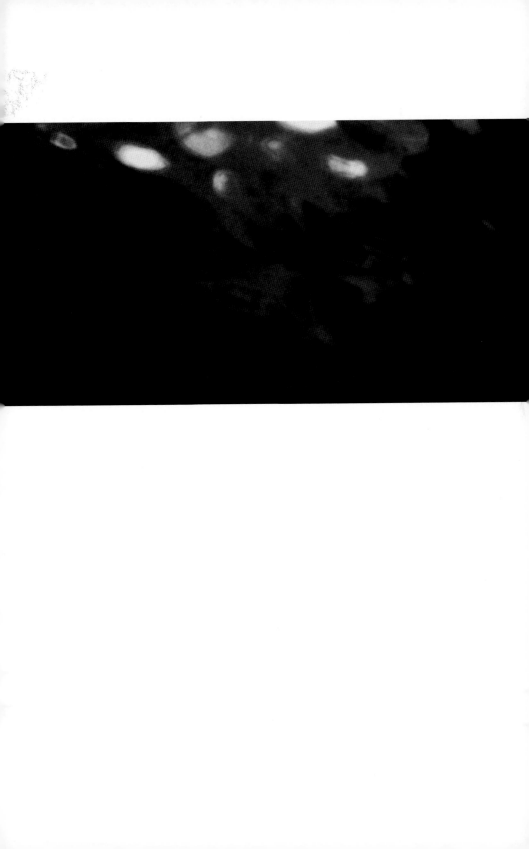

The Desire

They loved each other and, within days of meeting each other for the first time, they decided to marry.

Their wedding was a lavish celebration.

Their feelings of love and happiness spread to everyone in the city.

With each passing day, their love grew. In spring, they would open the windows of their home and allow the fragrance of blossoming flowers to fill their home. In summer, they would swim in the deep

waters of the lake. In autumn, they would walk together through the paths in the forest. In winter, they would run, laughing, through the snow.

After a few years, she became ill. As a physician, he did all that he could to save her. But it was clear to both of them that she would soon die.

One day, she called to him. She held his hand firmly and asked him to be strong. She asked him to continue to live happily for both of them. He wept as he listened, but he could not understand what she asked. She begged him to agree, which he reluctantly did.

She died that night.

Sadness overcame the city. He wept throughout the funeral. He thought about her request to him, which caused him to miss her more deeply.

Years passed, and he remained alone. He would call out to her in the mountains, on the forest paths, across the waters of the lake. He wept for her to return. Soon, all sense of happiness left his heart. He became bitter. His patients stopped visiting his office, his friends stopped inviting him to go out. Their home began to fall apart. The window shutters broke, the walls began to crack. But he did not care. Life for him had become only bitter sadness.

There were moments he would feel her presence near to him, but when he would look over his shoulder, there was no one there. His bitter sadness deepened.

One summer night, as he sat weeping, a strange sound whistled in the trees outside of their home. He stood up and walked to the front door. He looked out and saw her there. Small blue flames floated around her. He could not move.

She approached him, saying that she had been trapped between this world and the next. She had wandered for many years, searching for him. She was finally allowed to return to him, to tell him that his sadness was keeping her trapped. He needed to let her go freely to the next world.

He told her that he had not wanted her to die. That he wanted her to stay with him. She told him that he must accept what had happened, and that he must continue to live. He asked to join her. She replied that he could not, that it was not yet time for him to enter the next world. He pleaded to her. He insisted.

She quietly took him by the hand and walked him into the skies above. Together, they crossed many canyons of stars and shadows. They crossed deserts of ice and jungles of stone.

He tried to speak to her but no words left his mouth.

She turned to him and spoke, but there was no sound.

He could hear nothing and say nothing.

They were within a pure silence.

She placed her lips to his. He trembled as they kissed.

She then motioned for him to return to their home.

He wept as he began to walk alone. His tears formed currents through the jungles and storms in the deserts.

He turned to see her ascend to the sky. The blue flames that had surrounded her fell away, forming showers of light in the darkness of space.

When he returned, he found their home lit in blue light falling from above.

After many years, he smiled, knowing she was with him again.

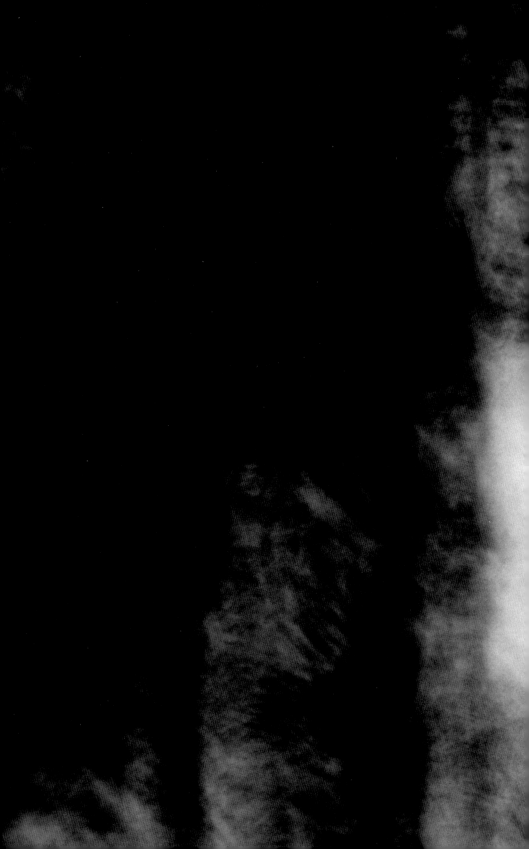

The Wind

No one knows when the strange wind first began. Some say it has blown across these lands for countless centuries. Others say that it started recently, during the horrific reign of the eighth emperor.

What is certain is that when the wind begins to blow, everyone in the surrounding area knows to go indoors and close all of the shutters on the windows. Everyone knows not to look outside.

The wind always starts off gentle, then picks up speed and force, until the only sound that is heard is the howling and rushing of the wind.

It has been recorded that horrid things happen to those who are caught in the wind - madness, illness, death.

The young woman and her son had just arrived to the town. They had moved to the town from an outer province.

It was a hot summer evening, and their first night to sleep in their new home. Their home was small but the woman was pleased to be starting a new life in this town.

The little boy began putting his things away in his room - his books, art supplies and toys.

She began putting their dishes in the small cabinet in the kitchen.

The wind began to move slowly through the trees. The sound of the wind began as a faint growl, then grew louder. The little boy heard the strange sound and looked out of his room window. The wind then began to blow with force that shook the window. He stepped back, afraid, yet curious of the sound. He looked out of the window again and saw the outlines of faces through the trees. The faces were very pale and howled in the wind. Some of the faces pressed against the window.

The little boy screamed and ran to his mother in the kitchen. The wind slammed harder against their house, rattling the wooden beams of the ceiling overhead. Frightened, his mother quickly grabbed a table and attempted to bar the windows. The wind scraped at the front door and forcefully shook the windows of the house.

She suddenly remembered something she had heard as a small child: when a malevolent spirit approaches, write a prayer on one's hands to protect oneself from the spirit. She ran to the boy's room and took some of his art supplies.

Her hands trembled as she wrote a short prayer of protection on the palms of her son's hands. She then asked him to write the same prayer on her palms. When they had finished, they sat on the floor of the kitchen, listening to the wind clawing at their roof and scratching at their windows.

The wind burst through the kitchen window, shards of glass flying towards the little boy. She pushed him down flat on the floor and covered his body with hers.

Over and over, she told her son that they were protected. Shards of glass sliced over her, thin sharp sounds whistling by the boy's ears.

The wind clawed at the woman and the little boy, alone on the floor of their home.

After a time, the wind stopped.

The young woman and her son stood up. Except for the smashed kitchen window, all was the same as before.

The wind continues to lash out across the lands, across the houses, across the trees.

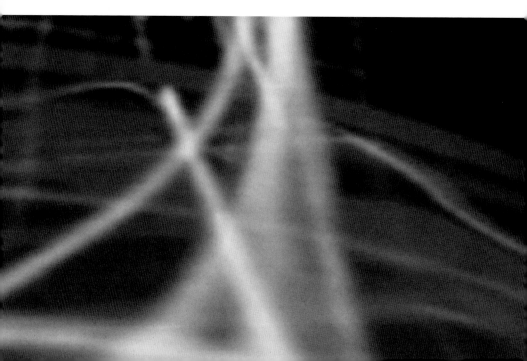

Blue Butterflies

The young girl and her mother were sitting under a tree, enjoying their afternoon meal.

The girl saw two blue butterflies flutter past, and she started to chase them. Her mother called out to her, but the girl continued running into the tall grass to get a closer look at the large butterflies.

The girl soon lost sight of the butterflies among the grass.

She tried to find her way out of the grass. She walked and walked but could not get out.

She heard her mother calling for her, and tried running towards her mother's voice, but she could not escape the grass. She ran through the grass in fear. She fell to her knees, sobbing.

The girl then heard a rustling behind her. She stood up and saw her mother standing among the tall grass with her arms outstretched. The girl ran to her mother, squeezing her in a relieved embrace. She was very happy to see her mother, but felt something different. Her mother embraced the girl tightly and did not speak.

The girl separated from her mother and looked at her mother's eyes. Her mother smiled and stretched out her arms for the girl to be hugged again.

But the girl felt something that frightened her. She started to run away from her mother.

She looked back and saw her mother, arms outstretched, running after her through the tall grass.

The girl finally found her way out of the grass. She looked back but did not see her mother anymore. She then heard her mother's voice calling to her. She ran and saw her mother, standing near the tree where they had been eating earlier.

Nearly out of breath, the young girl asked her mother why she did not speak to her when they were in the grass.

Her mother told her she had stood by the tree the whole time, calling out to her. Her mother had not gone into the grass.

Iemajaa

      I did not think I would survive. I had been struggling to stay afloat for what seemed like hours. I did not know how to swim at that time so I moved my arms and kicked my legs, trying to keep my head above the water. I saw the sinking boat and prepared my mind for the arrival of death. But death did not arrive. Instead, I was saved by the crew of the vessel that was responsible for sinking the ship I was on. The crew members said nothing as they hoisted me onto the deck of the large vessel. I had read about submarine vehicles, but I was not aware such a large type of submarine was possible. I was still dazed from my near-drowning as they took me into a

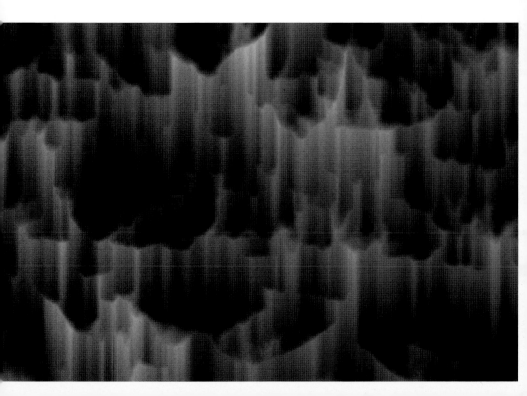

cavernous opening on the side of the vessel. Near the opening, I saw a large engraving in the steel hull of the vessel which read 'The Nautilus. 1876. Built by Nemo. With Gratitude and Praise to Iemajaa.'

I was treated well: a fire was made for me in one of the many rooms within the vessel. Food was brought and I ate heartily. I then fell into a deep sleep. When I awoke, I felt somewhat better and went out into the vessel I had been brought into. My room door led to an extensive hallway that curved inward beyond where I could see. Many passageways branched outward from it. I knocked on some of the doors along the hallway, but there was no response. I tried to open the doors, but all were locked. I walked for many minutes, following the curved shape of the hallway, which became more narrow the more that I walked. I did not see or hear anyone else. When I reached what seemed to be the end of the curved hallway, I saw a door with the letter N on it. I knocked but there was no response and the door was locked.

As I walked back to where I was brought in, I kept asking myself - Why was I brought onboard? Were others who were on the boat also saved? When I reached the cavernous opening, I saw a large, angled glass window that looked out into the ocean. The Nautilus was completely submerged, and we were descending even further into the water! I thought that all of the crew must be in the engine rooms and steering this large vessel. I then heard footsteps approaching, echoing off of the steel above me. A door opened near the window and an older gentleman stepped out followed by two younger crew members. They were all very dark-skinned men, but it was difficult to tell what exact country they were from. The younger men greeted me in my language: I noticed a slight accent which I could not identify.

The older gentleman looked into my eyes, saying nothing for a moment. I assumed he was the Captain of the Nautilus. His stare was frightening and I looked away. He laughed, saying, "I know you, more than you know yourself!" He shook my hand and walked back through the door, closing it behind him.

The two crew members took me back to the room I was first placed in. They turned a switch which opened the steel wall to reveal a small round window that looked out into the ocean water. I asked them, "Why am I here?"

One of them replied, "He wants you here. He saved you for a reason."

"But what about everyone else on the boat? Are they all dead? Did he kill them?" I yelled.

"He does not kill for sport. There is meaning in his actions. Good night, Professor." They left me alone in the room. On my first night aboard the Nautilus, I sat in my cabin watching the sea creatures in the water outside of my window until I fell asleep.

I slept for most of the first few days. Meals were brought to me in my cabin. I was allowed to walk along the curved hallway, but was not allowed to enter any other room or passageway. Sometimes on my walks, I would see a crew member. When I would ask one of them a question, they would all reply by saying the same thing - they would tell me

to save all questions for the Captain. I would desperately try to listen through the walls and doors along the hallway for any sound, but I could not hear anything. Finally, after a week, I heard a noise which sounded like a deep intake of breath. I looked outside my window and saw that the Nautilus was above the water. I could see bright sunlight reflecting on the surface of the water. I rushed out of my cabin and found Captain Nemo approaching me. "I'm glad you are well. Please join us for some fresh air," he said to me. I was confused, but I followed him through a passageway which led to a massive staircase that wound upward to the open-air deck at the top of the Nautilus.

The view was beautiful: clear sunlight, dark ocean waves, sea creatures jumping out of the water, seabirds flying overhead. I turned to see hundreds of people around me, also enjoying this moment. There were men, women and children. Everyone looked somewhat similar, but they had variations of skin tones, some people were lighter, some were darker. They would look at me and smile, welcoming me to the Nautilus. They told me this was their home! I was very confused by all of this and looked for the Captain, who was speaking with a group of elderly women.

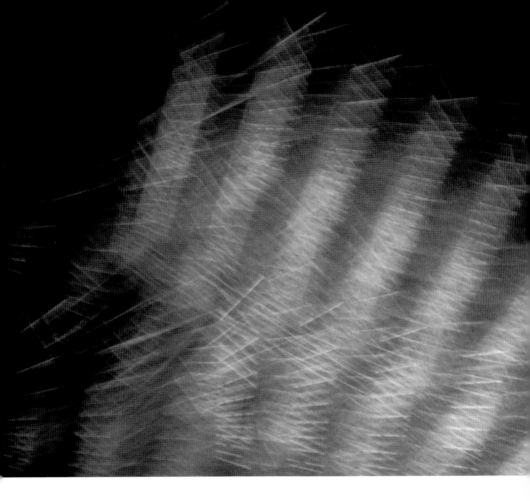

"Excuse my interruption, Captain Nemo, but I must speak with you immediately," I said.

The Captain excused himself to the women and motioned me to follow him to the outer railing of the deck. We walked together. He then turned to me, saying, "Your name is Joseph Arrow. You are a professor of international cultures at Northern University, one of the most prestigious universities in the world. You have written five books. You are unmarried and have no living relatives. Is this all correct?"

"Yes, but how did you...." I stammered.

"I acquire information when necessary. And now it is necessary. It is true: I did bomb and destroy the boat you were on last week. You are the only survivor, because I saved you."

"You are a monster!" I screamed, trying to punch him. He swiftly moved out of the way of my fist and grabbed my arm, forcing me to the ground.

"I am no monster. I am justice that strikes out against those who destroy the land and enslave its people! I am the force that strikes against those who desecrate the memories of the ancestors!" Nemo stated, forcing my arm higher against my back.

I yelled out in pain, "What are you talking about? Why have you brought me here?"

"You are of native heritage, and yet you follow the way of life of the conquerors of your land. You live their twisted way of life. Your own past is a mystery to you. And you claim to teach culture to others?" he said, letting my arm loose.

I got up saying, "How do you know me?"

"You are as transparent as glass," he said, looking out to the ocean.

"What do you want from me?" I yelled.

"I brought you here, onboard the Nautilus, so that you can learn about us. After a time, you will go back to the land, back to where you are from. And you will tell the world all that you have experienced on the Nautilus. You will tell the world that we survive, that we live on our own terms, by our own methods. Tell them that we do not need them. Tell people around the world that another way of life is possible!" Nemo declared.

I glared at Nemo and asked, "How long must I be here?"

"As long as it takes," he replied, leaving me alone.

Anger was boiling inside of me. I looked out to the ocean. I could not see land in any direction. I turned and saw Nemo go back to the crowd of people who were beginning some type of celebration. I watched them from where I stood, seeing them prepare what looked like presents. Everyone was involved, wrapping, organizing small gifts. Everyone looked so happy, yet I was so confused: I had been saved to accomplish something for them, for myself. I needed to find out what the reason was. I decided to stay on the Nautilus until I found out.

The people on deck then began to throw the flowers and the gifts they had prepared into water of the ocean that surrounded us. Everyone cheered and sang as the gifts were cast into the ocean. After they were finished, a band started playing and the celebration continued. There was music, singing and dancing. A group of young women ran up to me and dragged me into the party: they started to teach me their dances. I smiled and started to let myself go. At one point I saw Nemo join the band, playing percussion. I could see that he was smiling. I thought about what Nemo had told me earlier.

Weeks passed. I made many friends with the people who lived onboard the Nautilus. I learned that they had come from various parts of the Earth, from various tribes: all of the people were of some type of native heritage. Nemo had found them all: he had saved them from battles or freed them from slavery. They had become his crew. In speaking with them, I learned that none of them had returned to land since Nemo found them. They had grown accustomed to living in the water. They did not long for the lands they had left behind. All of them were truly happy to live onboard the Nautilus. I realized that Nemo had assembled all of them to form a new society, a society that lived independently and autonomously in the oceans of the world. A society that lived free.

In those weeks, I also learned about the workings of the Nautilus. I learned that the vessel is powered by a gas found only in vents in the deepest parts of the ocean. Each week, the Nautilus must descend and refill its fuel tanks with gas from the vents. I was shown, by Nemo himself, how the Nautilus must also surface once a week, to renew its air supply. Nemo spoke very little, but I could see that he wanted me to comprehend what he had told me that day on the deck. I was starting to understand.

I discovered libraries, a theater, art museums and schools among the many chambers of the Nautilus. Everyone had access to the resources of the vessel. The artwork the people were creating was very beautiful and unlike anything I had ever seen or read about. I was frequently invited to events in the theater - storytelling, music concerts, performances, dances.

After two months, the Nautilus reached a very dark ocean. The water appeared black, even

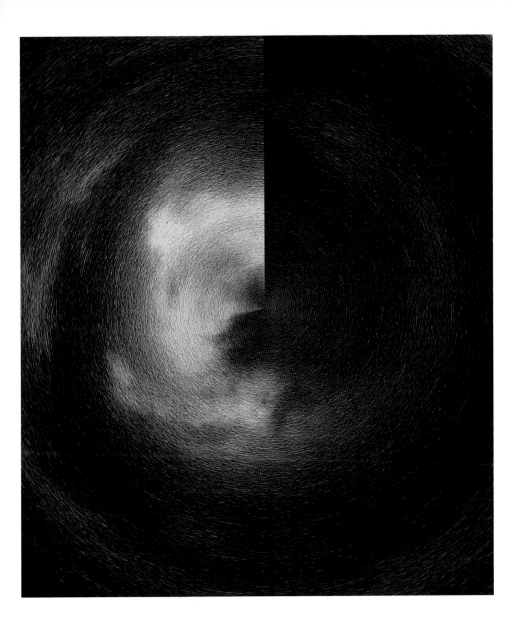

during the day. But at night, a bright blue light would arise from the deep waters. The blue light could be seen for many kilometers around us. Everyone onboard, including myself, felt a great sense of awe and inspiration in watching the light. One night I heard a rhythm reverberating through the Nautilus. I followed the sound until I reached the end of the hallway: the drumming was coming from the room on the other side of the door that was marked with an N. Suddenly, the drumming stopped and the door opened. Nemo stood at the door, welcoming me into his chamber. I could see panels of navigational instruments and reflector screens that showed the views from the front, back and sides of the Nautilus. Nemo resumed playing, losing himself in the rhythm. I enjoyed listening to the sound of the drums echo down the hallway of the Nautilus. Soon, other crew members entered and began playing their percussion instruments. Then dancers entered and began to move in time with the music. The festive atmosphere spread to everyone on the vessel until all was music and dancing.

The months passed quickly. I enjoyed learning many new things aboard the Nautilus. On days the vessel would surface, crew members would teach me how to swim: I learned quickly and soon did not fear the ocean water. A group of young women, who were teachers like myself, taught me some of the names and characteristics of the animals and plants that lived in the depths of the ocean. I learned about the system of caverns below the surface of the ocean that connects all of the Earth. My friends onboard the Nautilus built small vessels and took me on tours of undersea lakes, forests, volcanoes and canyons. They would guide me along the bottom of the ocean floor, all of us wearing iron suits and breathing through tubes of air. I learned to appreciate that the ocean is a world unto itself.

One afternoon, Nemo invited me to the main navigation chamber. There were numerous panels of levers, switches and reflector displays. I noticed some of the crew members seemed worried, but Nemo calmed them. I looked into a reflector display and saw what was worrying them: the Nautilus was approaching a swirling maelstrom! Nemo seemed very calm. He took control of the multi-levered panel and began navigating the vessel straight into the heart of the maelstrom! I was frozen in fear. I looked into another reflector display and could see an endless abyss directly below. I did not understand what Nemo's purpose was, but he calmly guided the Nautilus into the maelstrom We felt the vessel swirl slightly, then begin sliding rapidly downward, toward the abyss. I grabbed the railing of the chamber as I watched. After a few moments, the Nautilus straightened out and there was silence.

Nemo turned to me and said, "Arrow, look into the reflector display." I did as he requested and saw an amazing sight. It was the remains of an ancient city. I could see crumbling buildings, the layout of extensive gardens, the traces of carved writings on the walls of tall structures. "Some of my ancestors are from here. Some of your ancestors also," Nemo solemnly told me. "They were destroyed, by the people of the land. And now, this place and its people are spoken of only as myths. But they are real. We are real...." Nemo's voice became softer. "One day, we will construct entire cities under the oceans of the world. We will build these cities so that future generations will live free from the injustices and lies of the people of the land. We will build these cities so that, like onboard the Nautilus, people will live in the freedom of the ocean."

I had been onboard the Nautilus for ten months. I was sitting alone in my cabin, looking out to the rich sea life that was illuminated by the bright lanterns of the Nautilus. I started to realize that I had stopped thinking about land. I realized that I had grown accustomed to living in the water! I was shocked at this fact, yet I felt a sense of joy that I had never felt before. Just as I was thinking about this change I had experienced, I felt the Nautilus rising to the surface. I went up to the deck and saw that we were approaching land! I could see a large land mass before us. I turned to see Captain Nemo walking toward me. I asked him, "Where are we?"

"We are at the point that marks the beginning of your new life," Nemo said to me, shaking my hand. I watched as everyone who lived onboard the Nautilus came up onto the deck to bid me farewell. I wept as I said my farewells to all of them, the people I had become closer to than anyone else I had known before. I was given a small raft and reached the shore in a few minutes. I watched as the Nautilus descended back into the depths of the ocean.

I have built my life on land once again. Yet I am different. I feel, as Nemo had said to me, that I have begun a new life. I now understand Nemo's drive to create a society that lives free from those who live on land, free from those who continue to fight and conquer and enslave others. I now understand Nemo's plan to teach me that a complete, functioning and nurturing society is possible below the surface of the ocean. His bombing of my boat was despicable, but what despicable events had happened in his own life? What atrocities had Nemo himself experienced? What horrors had the crew members and the people onboard the Nautilus experienced? I will never know. But I have learned that another way of life is possible for all. And, as Nemo asked me, I will speak of this to people around the world.

Essence and Destiny

Space is a shadowy and fluctuating domain - condensing and expanding with the vacillating energies of the imagination

In time, newer planets will be found, some more luminous than those that are older and more remote

In time, luminous suns will be found, encircled by luminous and non-luminous rings, between which, revolve luminous and non-luminous planets, orbited by moons, which themselves will have moons

All in an endless system of cycles, an eternal stability, an eternal symmetry

In time, it will be found that all stellar bodies will merge into One and matter will disappear

But the Universe will not end

The processes will be renewed forever: a new Universe will swell into existence, then subside into nothingness followed by another sparking, flaming and extinguishing of a Universe

The continuous rhythm of One expansive existence

A new and different series of conditions will begin; another creation and radiation, returning into itself; another action and reaction of the One

All the creatures in the Universe, all individual intelligences, will become mixed into One

Each individual intelligence will absorb all other intelligences

Each will become One.

All will become One.

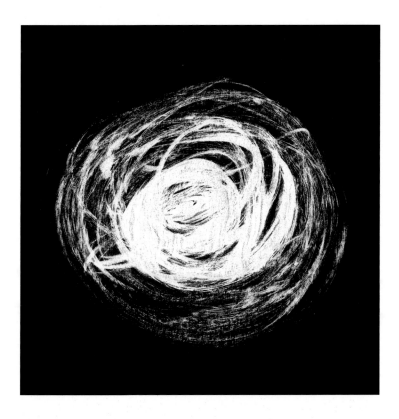

Its Eyes of Yellow Fire

Victor knew that he must build the being. It was inside of him, since he was a child. As a medical student, he knew there were things beyond science, beyond chemistry and numbers and texts. After many years of being a doctor to the wealthy people of the city, Victor quit his profession. He began designing the being. He wanted to create it so that it would live and walk as he did. So that it would breathe and speak, with Victor's thoughts inside of it. He wanted to live on through the being, so that after Victor himself was dead, the being would continue Victor's life.

Victor worked alone in his laboratory in the mountains. He drew out his designs and circuits and developed printing devices to plot out his diagrams. He accessed the most recent information on solar and electrical current technologies through his telegraphic lines.

Victor would go into the city once a week to collect all of the materials he required to build the being - human and animal organs and body parts, electrical wiring, mud pastes, solar panels. In his laboratory, he ran various tests on individual limbs and organs to check motor responses and functions, refining the accuracy of his design.

When Victor would go into the city, he would not speak to anyone. He did not care to have conversations about current events or about changes in the weather. He did not care for the latest advancements in steam-powered vehicles and devices, or ocean water power plants: he knew that his creation, the being, would prove to be the greatest achievement in human history.

The November sun hung behind dark clouds. Its fragmented light entered the laboratory windows as Victor began building the being. He assembled the organs and body parts on the large steel table. He laid the wiring throughout the various body parts and organs, then fused the pieces together, pasting it all into the shape of a human. He installed the electrical switches and relays in the being's head, connecting them to solar panels which ran across the being's scalp.

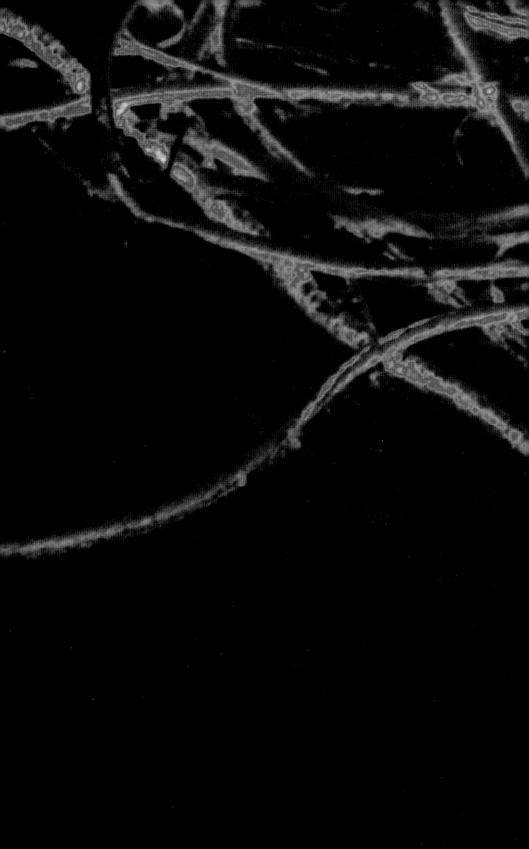

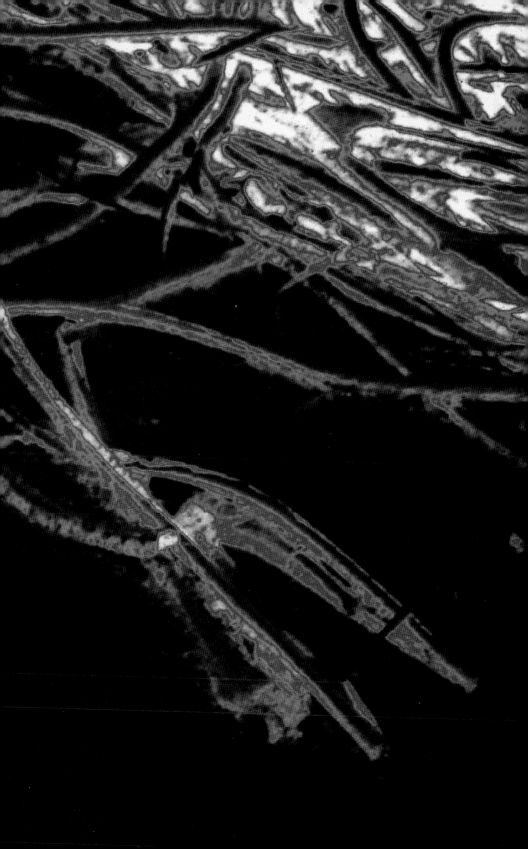

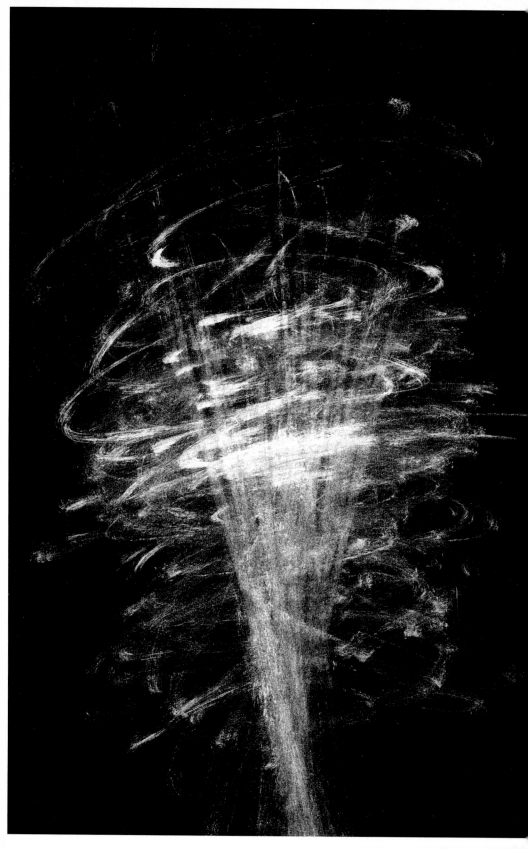

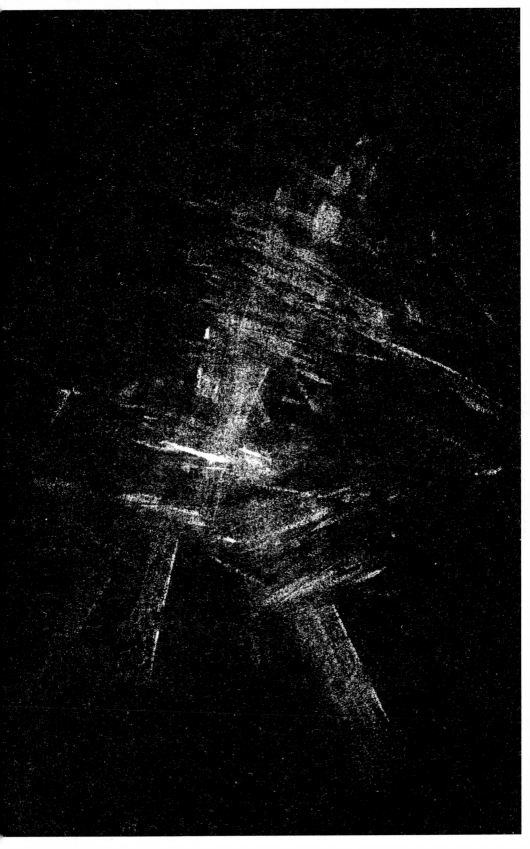

Victor adjusted the solar reflectors and connected the electrical current to two sockets on the being's neck. Sparks shot across the laboratory. Flames wrapped around the being's body. Victor switched the current on: the being convulsed. Its yellow eyes opened, burning within the thin layer of skin that covered its skull. The being looked straight into Victor's heart. Terrified, Victor jumped backward and stumbled, falling to the floor into a puddle of mud and coils. He stood up, looking at his creation in the eyes.

Victor's fingers trembled as he connected wires from the being's head to his head. The being continued to look at Victor. Victor said nothing as he switched on the relay program: Victor's thoughts began to fill the being's mind. Victor could see understanding start to fill the being's eyes. When the program was complete, Victor disconnected the wires and asked the being to stand.

The being shook as it lifted its body. It stood up and began to walk. It moved as a spider moves - deliberate, menacing. It caught its reflection in the window. The being looked at itself for a long time.

Victor asked it "How do you feel?"

The being turned to face Victor "Feel.... Feeling...."

"Do you understand what I am saying?"

"Yes. I can understand...."

"Do you know who I am?" Victor asked.

"Yes. You made me. Why have you made me?" the being asked, looking into Victor's eyes.

"I made you so that you can live. So you can know what it is to breathe, to think," Victor said proudly.

"To think? Whose thoughts are in my mind?" the being asked.

"Mine. You will carry my thoughts forward, into the future. You will live long after I have died," Victor stated triumphantly.

"Why will I carry your thoughts?"

"Because I have given you life."

"I did not ask to live," the being responded, looking at the decaying flesh of its arms. "I did not ask to be this."

"But you can create others like you, you can create an entire population of beings with your intellect. You can live through them."

"That is not life. This is not living. I am breathing, but I am an empty shell. This is your life. These are your thoughts," the being replied, slamming its palm against its forehead.

Victor saw the being's frustration and tried to ease it by saying, "You can build, you can create. I have given you a powerful gift."

"I do not want your gifts!" the being growled. It grabbed Victor by the throat and threw him into the corner of the laboratory. It smashed the door and ran into the mountains.

"I made you! I made you!" Victor cried out. Rain began to strike the walls of the laboratory. Victor looked out, seeing the being's silhouette ascend the ice-covered peaks.

Many years passed. Victor remained alone. He did not attempt to build another being. He burned all of his plans and diagrams, placing them into the fire. Yellow flames brightened the laboratory for an instant, then faded.

The being lived alone in the ice-covered mountains. It would frequently descend into the cities below the mountains, in a hooded cloak that covered its decaying features. The being would look into the faces of the humans. It saw their meaningless lives, their lack of love. Everything was emptiness. The being stole many books on various subjects: history, science, psychology. It learned of the viciousness of humanity. It learned of wars and the conquests of lands and people. The being walked through city streets, looking into each person's eyes, seeing only vileness. The more the being experienced humanity, the more it saw the wretchedness and pollution that humanity had created.

The being understood that humans would continue to destroy, that humans would one day destroy the earth itself.

Victor was alone in the laboratory, the yellow fire crackling in the winter air. Suddenly, Victor heard the outside door open. He heard the being approach, its heavy feet climbing the stairs. Victor stood up. Not saying a word, the being grabbed Victor by the throat. It squeezed until Victor's eyes were lifeless. The being then laid Victor's dead body on the large steel table.

The being sat down and began designing. It created its own design to bring life to Victor's corpse. The being smiled as it devised methods in which Victor's revived corpse would exterminate all of humanity. The yellow fire, in time, became ash.

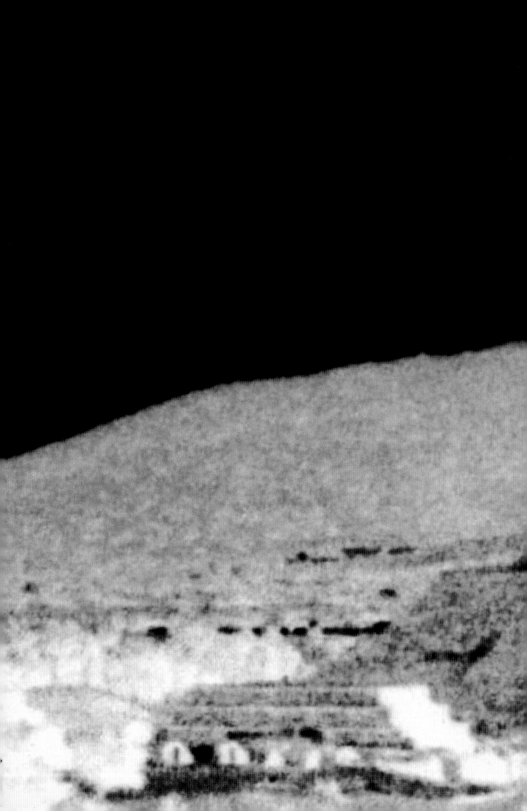

The Fourth World, The Fifth Sun

The seer had a warning for all of the tribes of the continent. She called together a meeting with the council of all tribal leaders. They met on the clearest night of the year, when the Earth is closest to the stars. She called for the meeting to take place on top of the pyramid at the center of the continent.

After the greeting ceremonies and celebrations, she began to tell the tribal leaders of the strange, long-legged men that would arrive soon to the continent. These men would come from across the oceans. These men would come to grasp the heart of the Earth, to squeeze out the blood from its core. She said they would come to steal the wind and to devour the grass, trees and animals of the Earth.

She told the tribal leaders that the long-legged men would replace their ancient tribal life with a withered husk.

She told them that every word that leaves the mouths of the long-legged men would be a lie. She said everything these men would perceive and create for themselves would be a lie. All would be gloom, misery and despair in the eyes of the long-legged men.

These men would bring many new things that they say would improve the lives of the tribal people; but these things would only distract and destroy the tribes.

She told the tribal leaders that the long-legged men would arrive soon and she advised the tribes to be vigilant, to resist their ways. She said, in time, it may be possible to teach the long-legged men how to speak with the Earth.

The tribes returned to their homelands - those from deserts returned to deserts, those from forests returned to forests.

And soon after, the tribes watched as large vessels approached the shores of the continent. The long-legged men arrived, dressed in metal and carrying fire. A shadow also disembarked from one of the boats, casting dark smoke into the air. The smoke was carried by the wind and formed a ring of dark clouds around the Earth.

The long-legged men built structures that blocked the sun from the Earth. The long-legged men built machines that blew smoke which was carried by the wind, expanding the dark clouds that encircled the Earth.

In time, mountains began to crumble. The many-colored arcs in the sky were shattered, shards of color falling across the land. The air became grey ash.

Illnesses spread to all of the tribes. Each tribe was renamed and divided.

All of the tribal leaders gathered again, on the pyramid at the center of the continent. They danced and sang, recalling the words of the seer. They danced to clear away the dark smoke that the long-legged men had brought with them.

The tribal leaders danced to call forth the return of the many-colored arcs in the sky.

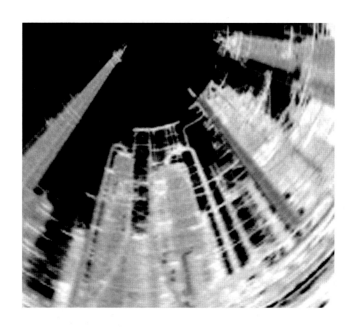

The Harmonics of Time

As I write this, moments pass - one crashing into another, as waves on a shore of a distant beach. One can remember childhood, or one's first kiss, or a multitude of memories carried by the waves onto the shore of that beach. And each memory will hold countless thoughts and emotions with it.

I write this in my studio, upon my return. I arrived back here to my studio after having been away only two days. Yet even to say "two days" seems odd now. Inaccurate. Time is now different than I had experienced before. Time is now...more important. Precious. Sacred. Time may seem cyclical, but it does not move in the same cycles as we might have expected. Time is surprising, I have learned.

Two days ago, I was making the final adjustments and calibrations on my time vehicle, my life's dream. I had always imagined traveling through time - seeing the movement of years in seconds, seeing centuries pass before me. Music filled my studio as I worked. The sound playing and recording device I had constructed as a young man continued to work very well. The sounds were crisp: each rhythm was clear as it traveled through the bass tubes and into the cool fall air of my studio. I had plans to continue to develop a series of sound playing and recording devices but as I grew, I began to focus more and more on my time vehicle. I smiled, glad I had decided to install the sound device into my time vehicle.

Drum sounds reverberated across the studio walls. Outside I could see the sun was setting. I worked faster. I ran into my study for my overcoat. I stepped back into my studio. The light of the setting sun struck the dark blue crystal of my time vehicle. I stood for a moment, watching the light

move across the edges of the machine which I had worked on for many years. The gold gears and blue crystals sparkled. Looking at the curvilinear shape of the vehicle, it seemed as if someone else had built it. It was as though I was seeing it for the first time.

I quickly entered the vehicle and stored the few things I was bringing with me on my first journey through time. I switched on the air compressors. Steam and smoke filled the studio. The drums beat loudly around me. I pressed the outer valves closed. I did not know what environment I would find in the future. I had built my time vehicle for land, air or water, so I would be prepared for various possible environments. I turned the silver calendar dials, setting them to 20,000 years forward from that day. I ignited the acceleration module and closed my eyes for what seemed to be a second. Light sparked around me, then darkness. Sounds echoed.

When I opened my eyes, I was floating on a dark ocean. The sun was a burning orange disc in the sky. I could not see land in any direction. Only thin mists above the surface of the water. I calculated my coordinates: I was exactly in the same place that I had departed from, yet I was not on land.

I turned on the sound recording device. I adjusted the lenses on the visual instruments to one kilometer, then five kilometers, then one thousand kilometers. I could not see land. The planet, it seemed, was now completely enveloped in water. I could see no structures or humans. I turned the visual instruments to the skies: I could see what appeared to be birds flying at high altitudes above the waters. The birds' shapes were varied, some large, some very small.

I submerged the visual instruments into the waters below my vehicle: beneath the water's surface was a lush atmosphere of plants and countless marine animals.

I decided to float for a day and activate the air flight formation the following day. In the sound playing device, I put on a slow multifrequency recording I had recorded as a greeting. I directed the bass and treble tubes of the sound device downward toward the water. I sent out these sonic signals to the verdant waterscapes below me. And I waited.

I watched the small fish animals react first, swimming away very quickly. Other larger fish also swam away at first but soon swam towards my vehicle in curiosity. Soon all animals quickly rushed away. I scanned the waters looking for the reason. Then I saw them. Large dolphin-like animals with long frontal flippers approached. It was a group of approximately 50 of them, swimming in parallel formations. They all stopped and simultaneously made a high-pitched sound. Then they swam around my vehicle, touching the steel hull. I could feel their tapping below my feet.

I stopped the sound playing device. The water creatures stopped tapping my vehicle. Excitement pulsed within me. Then an amazing occurrence: the creatures began tapping the hull of my vehicle in the rhythm of the recording! They had listened to the recording and learned the sonic patterns! I heard them play the song from the recording in its entirety. Then they began to do something which I can only describe as improvisation. One would begin to make high-pitched sounds, at first in key and in time with the notes and rhythm of the sound recording which I had played. Another creature would make sounds that would expand on the note pattern of the sound recording! Soon others would do the same, until all the dolphin-like creatures that were swimming around me were improvising based on the sound recording! Shivers ran through my spine as I listened to their music. These highly intelligent aquatic creatures had listened to the sound recording and were responding and improvising! I thought of a name for the creatures, calling them "aquaparali" because of their sonic harmonizing and for the way they swam in parallel formations.

They continued making their sounds, their music, and I focused my visual instruments to study their physical form. Their bodies were larger than dolphins I had seen at the World Expositions I had visited in my century - they were approximately 2 meters in length. Their heads were shaped similar to dolphins I had seen: their eyes were dark, they had blowholes on the top of their head area,

one row of small white teeth extended along their mouths and small ear openings on the sides of their heads. The most striking difference between the dolphins I had seen and the aquaparali were their flippers: the aquaparali had long frontal flippers and two short hind flippers.

They appeared to enjoy my presence and began swimming in many different formations, continuing to make their improvisational music. When I would move the lenses of the visual instruments in the water below my vehicle, the aquaparali would notice and swim back towards me. They would touch the lenses with their frontal flippers or their long beak-like mouth. I noticed that they would stare into the glass lenses of the visual device. They seemed to understand I was watching them and continued to swim into the depths and out of sight. Then they would return at high speeds directly towards the lenses. It seemed like they were playing a game! I quickly put a different song into the sound playing device, a faster tempo and multi-rhythmic piece, to see their reactions. Their enthusiasm seemed to increase! They began to swim even faster and to make sounds in time with the song. Soon, as before, they learned the various parts of the song and began improvising on the rhythms. I continued watching them and playing various music pieces throughout the day, until they all at once swam towards me: they all simultaneously made a high-pitched sound then swam together into the depths in the parallel formations. I understood that was the announcement of their parting.

I watched as smaller fish and marine creatures slowly returned to the waters below me. It appeared that the aquaparali were at the top of the food chain and all the other marine creatures feared them. The orange sun set in a blast of light in the sky. A white mist rose over the ocean and a full moon rose over the horizon. I watched until my eyes felt heavy. I pulled out the sleep chamber and entered. That first night I slept deeply. Countless dream images moved through my mind.

I awoke to birdlike sounds. Hundreds of birds were in the waters and in the skies, fishing, scouting, resting. They looked similar to birds I was familiar with: seabirds, birds of prey, small birds. I turned the visual instruments into the water and saw again the lush atmosphere of plants, fish and other marine animals. I could not see the ocean bottom. I turned the visual instruments back up towards the birds and pulled out a set of glass food tubes. I had breakfast while watching the birds' activities. The sun burned in the sky and felt warm through the crystal of my vehicle. After eating, I retrieved samples of the air and water outside. All the data showed that this environment was very similar to the environment in the time period I had come from yesterday. I decided to open the main overhead crystal vents. A blast of wind entered my vehicle: I grabbed onto a railing to brace myself. It soon subsided as the pressure inside my vehicle equalized to the outside. I climbed up and looked out to the ocean that surrounded me. I breathed in deeply. Clean, ocean breezes blew. The bird sounds were very loud now. The sky was clear, yet seemed a darker hue of blue. I looked all around, seeing water in every direction. I climbed back down and activated the air flight formation of my vehicle. The two wings extended and the engines lowered into the water. I turned the silver altitude dials to 500 meters and ignited the acceleration module. The acceleration was slow at first. Frightened, the birds all hurriedly flew away from my vicinity. I picked up speed and started rising above the water into the air. At 500 meters, I could see the densities of birds in every direction - all flying, resting on the water, diving into the depths, coming up with fish. But no land in sight. I turned the altitude dials to 1 kilometer. I noticed very large birds I had not seen before - each one was circling alone above the ocean. The cloud layers were thin. I could still see the vast waters below me. I then set the altitude dials to 20 kilometers and rose quickly to the higher atmosphere. The clouds were much thinner now. The sky seemed to be a deeper hue than before. I adjusted the acceleration module to 5 kilometers a

second. Wind blasted all around me and my vehicle quaked. I slowly lowered the speed and began descending again to see if I could view land. I continued like this for hours until I had circled the planet many times in many different directions. I did not see any land anywhere. As I had first thought, the entire planet had been completely inundated with water.

I descended back to the ocean level. Birds flapped out of the way of my vehicle. I landed smoothly on the surface of the water. I switched the engines for water movement and adjusted the pressure inside my vehicle. I switched on the outer lights along the hull and main windows.

The vehicle began descending smoothly through the dark waters. I stopped at the sight of ruins of buildings and bridges and structures, all covered in coral and plant life. I saw only marine life. I accelerated faster through the rows and rows of buildings and structures. There was no trace of human presence, only these ancient structures made by human hands.

Then they appeared again - the aquaparali. Hundreds, then thousands of them. Swimming along the

buildings, looking for food, playing, ascending to the surface for air. A large group of them approached my vehicle, making sounds from the recording I had played for them as a greeting yesterday. Had the aquaparali I "met" yesterday taught these others the song I had played for them as a greeting? Had all the aquaparali on this planet learned this song? I recorded their sounds as they began improvising as before. I adjusted the lenses on the visual instruments and some of the aquaparali touched them and stared into the lenses as others had done the day before. They also seemed to understand I was inside and seemed to call for me to look at them as they swam back and forth in the water. I could hear other aquaparali in the distance also making sounds in time with the recording I had played for them yesterday. I looked through the sound recordings I brought with me and chose another song with an intricate rhythm and played it for them through the sound device.

They all stopped making sounds for a brief moment while they listened and learned the various parts of the song. Then, as before, they began making sounds in time with the recording: and they began improvising! I listened in awe of these intelligent beings. An alarm went off: I had only few hours of air remaining within my vehicle. I stopped the sound device. The aquaparali continued making their music, swimming in many directions, continuing with their activities.

I needed to continue before resurfacing for air, I needed to see more of this underwater planet. I descended, further in the depths of the planet. The numbers of marine animal and plant life decreased the deeper I descended. I ultimately reached a depth of 20 kilometers, seeing the vast ocean floor. I began to theorize that the aquaparali were our descendants in the future! I thought about the shape of their bodies, of their intelligence, their communication, their social structures. Humans had returned to the sea, for some reason. We as humans had recreated our lives in the ocean. The ocean was now our home. And we seemed to enjoy what we and the planet had become. The alarm sounded once more: I had to return at once to the surface. I set the acceleration to 5 kilometers a second and rapidly reached the surface. I opened the main windows let in the ocean air once more. I directed the tubes of the sound device into the water. I played the same slow multifrequency recording I had played the day before as a greeting in the sound playing device. Again a large group of aquaparali approached my vehicle, playing in front of the visual instrument lenses, making sounds in time with the music, improvising, swimming, jumping in and out of the water around me. I stood at the main windows, seeing and hearing their joyous activities. I called to them in gratitude: their sounds grew louder and happier. I closed the main windows and prepared the vehicle for the next journey.

I turned the calendar dials to 5 billion years backward from that day. I activated the acceleration. Light blasted around my vehicle. Sounds ripped at the wind. I was in a vast mountain range, surrounded by volcanoes rumbling and erupting. The sky was a deep blue above. Countless stars were visible yet the sun was high in the sky. I could see legions of animals of all sizes, their sounds rising above the rumbling of the volcanic activities. I could see an ocean shore in the horizon. I realized this was the beginning of this planet! The lava erupting from the volcanoes began to approach the edge of the stone formation I was on.

I quickly set the calendar dials to 10 billion years forward from that day and accelerated. Colors burst around me. I was in a desert-like landscape. The sun was very large and close in the sky. Flames shot out from the sun, scorching the edge of this planet. There was no creature or living thing in any direction. I knew this was the moment the entire planet would be consumed by the sun. I watched as flames whipped into the horizon, this planet reaching its end. I set the calendar dials back to the time I had come from.

I arrived back to my studio. Everything was as I had left it. The sun was setting. I trembled as I stepped out of my time vehicle. I lied down and slept for what must have been days. Then I began to write this. I leave the various sound recordings I made of the aquaparali. I leave this written account of my adventures through time, for others to discover the possibilities and the wonders that we are born from, and the wonders that await us.

And now, it is time for another journey....

THE MULTIPLE ENTRANCE by Gustavo Alberto Garcia Vaca

Produced by Alma Villegas
Art direction and design by Hideki Nakajima
Published by chamanvision: www.chamanvision.com
Printed and bound in Japan by Toppan Printing Co., Ltd.

ISBN-10: 0-9749357-2-7
ISBN-13: 978-0-9749357-2-0

The Multiple Entrance is written and illustrated by writer / visual artist Gustavo Alberto Garcia Vaca, the creator of the critically-acclaimed Interstellar Transmissions and The Hidden Infinities books. His writing is published in science fiction / cyberpunk / slipstream magazines, books and literary anthologies. His artwork is exhibited in art galleries and museums around the world, including the Museum of Emerging Science and Innovation in Tokyo, Japan. His photography is published in various art books, including Graffiti World: Street Art from Five Continents. He collaborates visually with Detroit Techno record labels Los Hermanos and Jeff Mills' Axis Records; Francois K's Deep Space dub record label; and others.

Thank you:
The spirits throughout the Universe, mami, nuestras familias, Jeff Mills, Mike Banks, Yoko Uozumi, Axis Records, Hideki Nakajima, Takenobu Iino, Kiyoshi Takami, Nakajima Design, Thomas Hummel, Ikuo Hikida, Toppan Printing, Nomadico, Gerald Mitchell, Los Hermanos, Ade Mainor, Bridgette, Submerge, Juan Atkins, Metroplex, Ray 7, DJ 3000, Underground Resistance, Jowcol Music, Crewest Gallery, Alex, Overton Loyd, George Clinton, Harleigh Cole, Unification Theory, Kiwamu Omae, Kaze magazine, Ishizaki, Rie, Maria, Underground Gallery, Chifu, Ume, Mita, Disk Union Shibuya, Keiko Hoshikawa, Cisco Techno Shop, Kenji Kajimura, Shinichiro, Soundscape, Francois K, Aurelie, Wave Music / Deep Space Media, Yasuhiro Nara, Hirofumi Kiyonaga, soph.net, Yurika, Pedro Alonzo, Art Data, la familia Trochez, la familia Mazón, la familia Ortiz, the Cole / Ernsdorf family, the Brechtel family, the Omae family, Chaz Bojorquez, Christina Ochoa, nina, Kozo, Sumika, John Carr, Mari, Murata, Takeshi Mochida, Akira, Art Crimes, Justin, Emiko, Yuka Sudo, Brent Rollins, Ishiura Masaru, Rafael Castro, Kadija Sesay, Nii Ayikwei Parkes, the Museum of Emerging Science and Innovation, all the writers / music artists / visual artists whose work is a source of inspiration, and to you.